Barbie™ Wint Wonderland

By Rebecca Frazer • Illustrated by Karen Wolcott
Cover photography by Willy Lew, Shirley Fujisaki,
Julia Raylow, Doug Elliston, Steve Toth, and Judy Tsuno

A Random House PICTUREBACK® Book
Random House 🏠 New York

BARBIE and associated trademarks and trade dress are owned by, and used under license from, Mattel, Inc.
Copyright © 2007 Mattel, Inc. All Rights Reserved.
Published in the United States by Random House Children's Books, a division of Random House, Inc.,
New York, and in Canada by Random House of Canada Limited, Toronto.
No part of this book may be reproduced or copied in any form without permission from the copyright owner.
PICTUREBACK, RANDOM HOUSE, and the Random House colophon are registered trademarks of Random House, Inc.
Library of Congress Control Number: 2007924580   ISBN: 978-0-375-84222-1
www.randomhouse.com/kids   Printed in the United States of America   10 9 8 7 6 5 4 3 2 1

It was almost Christmas, and the whole town was getting ready! Barbie loved all the brightly decorated streets and store windows. She couldn't wait to decorate her own Christmas tree—especially since her friends were coming over for a tree-trimming party!

"Hey, Barbie!" someone called. It was her friend Ken. "Are you getting ready for the party?"

"Just doing some last-minute shopping," Barbie replied. "You're still bringing over the Christmas tree, right?"

"I have a few errands to run," Ken said. "But afterward I'll pick up the tree and take it to your house."

"Thanks, Ken!" Barbie said. "See you later!"

Barbie stopped by the Christmas Shoppe to pick up some extra decorations. Suddenly, an especially sparkly ornament caught her eye.

"My friends will love this," Barbie said as she handed it to the saleswoman. "I'll take it!"

"Merry Christmas!" said the woman as Barbie left the shop.

Barbie wanted to wear something special for the holidays, so she visited her favorite boutique, the Dream Closet.

"I love *all* these outfits," she said. "It's hard to choose just *one!*"

But when she spotted a soft red coat with a fluffy white collar, Barbie knew it was perfect!

Back home, Barbie and her sisters went straight to work.
They wanted everything to be just right for the party.
Skipper and Stacie made popcorn garlands . . .

. . . Barbie and Kelly baked cookies . . .

. . . and they all unpacked
the Christmas ornaments.

Barbie glanced out the window and couldn't believe her eyes. It was snowing!

"I love snow on Christmas Eve," she said.

"Everything looks so beautiful," Kelly agreed.

Barbie couldn't wait for her friends to arrive!

Ring! It was Ken. "I'm sorry, Barbie, but it's a blizzard out there. All stores are closed and the roads are blocked. I won't be able to get the tree. And I don't think we can make it to your party tonight."

Barbie was disappointed that she wouldn't get to spend Christmas Eve with her friends, but she didn't want them getting stuck out in the storm.

Barbie, Skipper, Stacie, and Kelly bundled up and went outside to enjoy the beautiful winter day. They weren't going to let the blizzard ruin their fun!

First Barbie made a pretty snow angel.

Then the sisters built a chubby snowman.
"Now your outfit is perfect!" Barbie giggled as she put
a hat on their cool new friend.

After enjoying the snow, they all went back inside to warm up. They wrapped themselves in blankets and sat in front of a roaring fire.

Knock! Knock!
"Who could that be?" Barbie asked.

"Merry Christmas!" everyone shouted when Barbie opened the door.

Barbie was surprised to see all her friends! They had come on snowshoes, a snowmobile—and even a snowplow!

Everyone went inside and sat around the fire, drinking hot cocoa and eating Christmas cookies.

"It's too bad the roads are blocked and the Christmas tree store is closed," said Ken. "It's a great night for a tree-trimming party."

Barbie looked out the window and smiled. "I have an idea," she said. "Follow me!"

"Let the tree-trimming begin," called Barbie as she led her sisters and friends to the big pine tree in the front yard.

Everyone sang and laughed as they hung ornaments and garlands and added their own special touches to the tree.

"It's beautiful," Carrie said, beaming. "But something is missing."

"How about this?" Barbie asked, carrying out the special decoration she had bought earlier that day.

With a sparkly star shining brightly at the top, everyone thought it was the most beautiful tree they had ever seen.

"Holidays are always special," said Barbie. "But they are extra special when you share them with people you care about. Merry Christmas, everybody!"

"Merry Christmas, Barbie!"